KU-685-514

Amy Johnson

Eva Bailey

Illustrated by
Julian Puckett

Hamish Hamilton
London

Titles in the Profile *series*

Edith Cavell	0-241-11479-9	Montgomery of Alamein	0-241-11562-0
Marie Curie	0-241-11741-0	The Queen Mother	0-241-11030-0
Roald Dahl	0-241-11043-2	Florence Nightingale	0-241-11477-2
Thomas Edison	0-241-10713-X	Emmeline Pankhurst	0-241-11478-0
Anne Frank	0-241-11294-X	Pope John Paul II	0-241-10711-3
Elizabeth Fry	0-241-12084-5	Anna Pavlova	0-241-10481-5
Indira Gandhi	0-241-11772-0	Prince Philip	0-241-11167-6
Gandhi	0-241-11166-8	Beatrix Potter	0-241-12051-9
Basil Hume	0-241-11204-4	Lucinda Prior Palmer	0-241-10710-5
Amy Johnson	0-241-12317-8	Viv Richards	0-241-12046-2
Helen Keller	0-241-11295-8	Barry Sheene	0-241-10851-9
John Lennon	0-241-11561-2	Mother Teresa	0-241-10933-7
Martin Luther King	0-241-10931-0	Queen Victoria	0-241-10480-7
Nelson Mandela	0-241-11913-8	The Princess of Wales	0-241-11740-2
Bob Marley	0-241-11476-4		

HAMISH HAMILTON CHILDREN'S BOOKS

Penguin Books Ltd, 27 Wrights Lane, London W8 5TZ (Publishing & Editorial)
and Harmondsworth, Middlesex, England (Distribution & Warehouse)
Viking Penguin Inc., 40 West 23rd Street, New York, New York 10010, U.S.A.
Penguin Books Australia Ltd, Ringwood, Victoria, Australia
Penguin Books Canada Limited, 2801 John Street, Markham, Ontario, Canada L3R 1B4
Penguin Books (N.Z.) Ltd, 182-190 Wairau Road, Auckland 10, New Zealand

First published in Great Britain 1987 by
Hamish Hamilton Children's Books
Copyright © 1987 by Eva Bailey
Illustrations copyright © 1987 by Julian Puckett

British Library Cataloguing-in-Publication Data:
Bailey, Eva
Amy Johnson. – (Profiles).
1. Johnson, Amy – Juvenile literature
2. Air pilots – England – Biography
– Juvenile literature
I. Title   II. Series
629.13'092'4   TL540.J58
ISBN 0-241-12317-8

Typeset by Pioneer
Printed in Great Britain at the
University Press, Cambridge

Contents

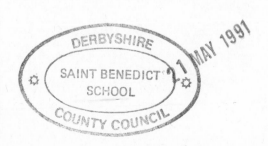

Amy Johnson

1   The Yorkshire Girl

In 1903, the American brothers, Wilbur and Orville Wright, made history by flying the first powered aeroplane. In that same year, Amy Johnson was born in Yorkshire. No one imagined on her birthday, 1st July 1903, that baby Amy would become a famous aviator.

Amy's family lived in Kingston-upon-Hull, but had no connection with flying. In 1881, her grandfather had founded a firm trading in herrings and salmon from Scandinavia and selling salted haddock and cod abroad. Amy's father was now the head of this prosperous firm of fish merchants, and the family lived very comfortably. Eventually Amy had three younger sisters, Irene, Molly and Betty.

Amy was mischievous and adventurous. She was only three when she turned up at a neighbour's house and announced that she had run away 'to be a queen'. The friendly neighbour promptly marched the protesting Amy back home.

Her love of wandering and travel showed in a much more carefully planned escapade a few years later. She bought some sweets, travelled a little way by bus and then walked until her legs were tired. However, Amy

Amy, as a girl

did not get far, because a friend of the family saw her as he was driving past, guessed what her plan was, and took her straight home.

Amy attended various small schools until she was twelve, when she was sent to the Boulevard Senior School. She loved boys' games and joined in enthusiastically at cricket and hockey. During a cricket match, the hard ball hit her in the mouth, breaking her front teeth. Amy's good looks were spoiled, and the denture she had to wear made her feel embarrassed. She became shy, often preferring to be on her own, but her love of adventure still persisted.

Straw boaters were part of the school uniform and Amy hated them. She persuaded her mother to buy her a soft panama hat like those worn at her sister's school. With the Boulevard badge fastened to the panama,

Amy wore the hat to school. She hoped others would follow her example, but they only laughed when they saw her, wearing the hat, standing outside the Head's room waiting to be reprimanded.

Amy's school results were patchy because she only worked at subjects which interested her. Because she was often late and sometimes played truant, she was not made a prefect. However, she did work hard to pass her University Entrance Examination.

When she was offered a place at Sheffield University, Amy accepted, then began to enjoy the summer holiday. Outings, films and tennis were all part of her programme. Earlier in the year, Amy's aunt had introduced her to a young Swiss businessman and, by the time she went to University, Amy was deeply in love.

At Sheffield University, there were others far more able than Amy and she did not get on well with her fellow students. She changed her lodgings often until, finally, she lived by herself in a tiny cottage in the moorland village of Hathersage.

Like most students, Amy had to budget her money. Usually she was careful, but occasionally she spent extravagantly, especially if she saw some lovely clothes. Debates, rag weeks, dramatics and dances filled Amy's university life and she played hockey for the First Eleven.

Amy left no time for study and failed her end-of-term examinations. She was in disgrace, but was given a second chance. She was dismissed from the honours course, but allowed to study for the ordinary Bachelor of Arts degree.

Amy did more work but still wrote long letters to her Swiss boyfriend and occasionally met him. As the third year final examinations approached, Amy's father came to discuss plans for her career but nothing was decided. Perhaps when he was in America, Father would get her a post there? Amy dreamed of travelling abroad, but her secret hope was that her boyfriend would ask her to marry him and whisk her away.

The dates of her examinations were announced and Amy worried in case she should fail again. In the examination hall, she struggled through the questions as if she was having a nightmare. When the results were announced she relaxed — she had gained her Bachelor of Arts degree.

Amy's mother wisely insisted that she should spend a few days at the seaside. After the holiday, Amy took a brief, concentrated secretarial course and then looked

Amy's parents, Mr and Mrs Johnson

for a post. With some difficulty, she found work with a chartered accountant. The office girls resented this confident young woman with her university education, whose shorthand speed was far too slow and whose typing was careless. The office job was a disaster and Amy had a nervous breakdown.

Mr and Mrs Johnson planned to send Amy to Bournemouth for six weeks' rest. In her vivid imagination, Amy pictured herself spending her leisure time in a luxurious hotel. She bought expensive clothes for this exotic life, but was heart-broken to learn that she was to stay with distant relatives at their home. Amy enjoyed herself in Bournemouth, however, and felt fit and well by the time she returned.

Amy found a new post as a copywriter in an advertising agency. She worried again because she could not pay the bill for the extravagant clothes she had bought, but did not dare to ask her father for help. She was grateful when her boyfriend settled the debt and eventually she repaid the loan from her earnings.

About this time, Amy first went up in an aeroplane and took her sister Molly for a 'Five bob flip'. For five shillings (25p) each, passengers were given a three minute flight. Amy imagined herself regally sailing through the air with a debonair pilot at the controls. In reality there was a lot of noise and a sickening smell of petrol and burning oil, while the wind pricked Amy's eyes and blew knots into her hair. Even the pilot had oil-stained clothes and dirty hands. Amy was very disillusioned, and the flight seemed to be over before it had begun. Perhaps her ideas were coloured by frequent visits to the cinema, where she loved watching romantic films.

Although Amy found the advertising work more interesting, she did not really settle. Business was bad at the agency, so Amy decided to go to London and find employment there. That was even more difficult than in Hull, and in desperation she joined a Learnership Scheme at Peter Jones, a London department store. Amy thought she was on a month's trial for a managerial post, but found it was for sales girls. After working for three weeks, Amy caught influenza and did not go back.

She was now alone in London with no wage to keep herself. She *must* get a post or she would starve. A cousin introduced her to Crocker's solicitors and, after an interview, Amy was offered a post. She was to be a typist, with the chance of promotion after gaining some legal experience. At last, Amy was content with her work, and greatly respected her boss, Vernon Wood.

Amy's love affair slowly fell apart. The couple quarrelled when they met, but Amy wrote lovingly when they were apart. When she received a letter mentioning her boyfriend's 'new friend', she knew something must be done. In a carefully-worded reply, Amy ended the association.

She filled her life with other activities in order to forget, but six months later the final blow came. Her Swiss boyfriend came to London, took her to lunch, and gently told her he had married someone else.

2　The Student Of Aviation

Amy could not forget her former boyfriend and at first her life seemed empty, but she was not going to let disappointment and sorrow spoil everything. Gradually she began to change from being calm and placid into a more determined, even aggressive person.

She decided to enjoy herself as much as possible. She joined the local tennis club, bought new clothes, went to the cinema and collected popular jazz records of the day, but none of these activities really satisfied her. Amy wanted to achieve something that was more worthwhile, but what? Where could she join a club that would give her an unusual outdoor activity?

It was after a holiday that Amy made the decision that was to change her life. She decided that she would learn to fly. She was to discover, however, that this was not going to be so easy.

At that time, only a few men were able to take part in this fairly new, risky pursuit, and the small number of women who were interested were not really welcomed. Flying lessons were expensive, but Amy was very keen. 'I will fly,' she promised herself, 'I'll succeed somehow.'

Geoffrey de Havilland was a prominent designer of aeroplanes. His factory for building aircraft was at Stag

Lane Aerodrome near Edgware, on the outskirts of London. Here he also ran the de Havilland School of Flying. Full of eagerness, Amy wrote to the school to find out as much as she could.

She was disappointed because the cost of flying lessons was higher than she expected. The duration of each flying lesson varied, but when the instruction time totalled one hour, a charge of £5 was made. Amy earned £5 a week, which was a good income at that time, but not enough for her to afford the expensive flying lessons. Despite this setback, Amy's interest in aeroplanes and the longing to fly did not go away.

One Saturday afternoon in April 1928, Amy boarded an open-topped bus and sat on the top deck so that, as she neared Hendon, she could watch the aeroplanes flying to and from the aerodrome. She stayed on the bus and travelled further, only getting off when she arrived at Stag Lane Aerodrome.

Amy walked around until she came to the entrance. It looked very private. She could see a group of people standing near a small wooden building, but no one came to see why she was at the gate. Amy decided to go in and joined the crowd watching the aeroplanes taking off and landing.

The flimsy aircraft soared and swooped. Amy was fascinated and, in her excitement, she started chatting to a pilot who stood nearby. He thought she belonged to the aeroplane club, so Amy had to admit that she was not a member.

To Amy's surprise and delight, the pilot told her that it only cost £3-3-0d (£3.15p) to join the London

Aeroplane Club, plus the same amount for each year's subscription. Lessons taken in the Club's aircraft were 30/- (£1.50p) an hour, much less than those at the de Havilland School on the same site. Amy also discovered that, after lessons totalling about eight hours, it was possible to take a test to get a pilot's certificate.

Amy lost no time. Within a week she became a member of the Club and started to save up to pay for the lessons. She was going to learn to fly!

Her elation turned to dismay as her name was put at the end of a long waiting list. Amy had imagined she would fly straightaway, but the club only had a few aeroplanes and there were not many instructors.

About five months passed before it was Amy's turn to have flying lessons. At last, on 15th September 1928, she stood beside a frail-looking biplane. She put on a flying helmet. It was too big, but Amy tugged at the strap and buckled it as tightly as she could. Then she adjusted her goggles.

Amy scrambled into the deep seat of the rear cockpit of the tiny Cirrus II Moth. Captain Matthews, her instructor, was in the front cockpit. These aeroplanes were built for men, not women, and being only 5ft 4in (160 cm) tall, Amy found that the only thing she could see was the back of the instructor's head.

As the plane began its steady climb up into the air, Amy was quivering with excitement.

Now that they were airborne, Amy's lesson began. There were dual controls on the aircraft so that, if the pupil was not able to handle it properly, the instructor could take over the flying of the plane at any time.

Flying instructors at the London Aeroplane Club

Amy's helmet had earphones fitted inside so that she could obey Captain Matthews' instructions. Because the helmet was too large, the earphones were in the wrong place, and Amy could only just hear the muffled voice of Captain Matthews. It was very difficult for her to understand what he was saying.

The first lesson was not a success. Captain Matthews was not impressed with Amy's efforts.

'You are no good,' he told her. 'You will never learn to fly.'

Amy went home to the flat she shared with her friend, Winifred. She was furious, but she would not give up.

Other lessons followed with various instructors. Amy particularly enjoyed those with Captain Baker, the Chief Flying Instructor at the club, but her progress was hampered by the onset of winter weather, which made flying impossible. She was able to resume her lessons the following March, and Captain Baker began teaching her how to land an aircraft. Amy soon realised that this was both difficult and dangerous. Captain Baker encouraged her and, after a few more lessons, he promised that if she could make two good landings he would let her fly solo. Amy longed to take the plane up on her own and worked hard until she satisfied Captain Baker. On 9th June 1929, she made her first solo flight.

Amy was not content, however, with just flying. She also wanted to find out everything she could about aircraft. She became fascinated by the technicalities of aviation and was eager to learn aircraft engineering.

She ventured into the hangars where the ground engineers worked and watched them checking an aeroplane that had just come in after a flight. The men looked suspiciously at this young woman who trespassed into their workshops. They made it clear to her that she was not welcome, but Amy persisted. She spent her annual holiday visiting the hangars. Her constant questions were answered politely, but reluctantly.

'Is there anything I can do?' she enquired one day.

The men glanced around to find her a job, then asked her to sweep the very dusty floor. Amy quickly set about the unpleasant task and soon made sure the floor was clean and tidy. When the engineers saw that she would willingly help with simple but dirty jobs, they realised that she was genuinely interested. Her welcome became warmer and the ground engineers nicknamed her 'Johnnie'.

Amy still practised flying as much as she could, and

on 6th July 1929, she took her test for a Pilot's 'A' Licence. To her delight she passed and was issued with Licence 1979.

Amy was not faultless or self-satisfied. She knew she had to improve her landings and navigation, so she spent all her leisure time at the aerodrome. She also wanted to know how all the parts of an aircraft worked. The Chief Ground Engineer, Jack Humphreys, promised to help her to qualify as a ground engineer. Amy was thrilled, but there were problems.

The first thing she had to obtain before she could become a ground engineer was a Pilot's 'B' Licence which would allow her to be paid for work as a pilot. To get this, Amy had to fly a total of one hundred hours. How could she find the money to pay for all that flying time? Amy was still working at Crocker's, the solicitors. There did not seem sufficient time — or money — to do all that was necessary to get the Ground Engineer's Licence.

Amy wrote to her father in Hull and asked if he could help. At first, Mr Johnson hesitated, but he knew Amy was determined to become a professional pilot. Finally, he agreed that she could leave Crocker's and gave her a small weekly allowance to live on for the next six months. He also agreed to pay for her training.

As she gratefully read her father's letter, Amy looked at her hands. No longer did she see the neatly manicured nails of a London office girl. They were the rough, oil-stained hands of an aircraft mechanic.

In the hangars, the working hours were from 8 a.m.

Three of Amy's examiners

to dusk, and Amy spent as much time there as she could. Wearing workman's overalls, she shared the jobs of stripping and cleaning engines, adjusting and rebuilding parts, and then testing them. Although Amy spent many hours in the workshops, she also did as much flying and studying as she could.

The time sped past, and the day of her Ground Engineer's Licence Examination arrived. On 10th December 1929, Amy Johnson presented herself to five examiners seated in a room at Stag Lane Aerodrome. They fired their questions and Amy gave her answers. It did not seem real and, as she came out of the examination room, Amy was uneasy. Had she thought the questions too simple? Were there deeper points she had not recognised?

3 Can Dreams Come True?

'I've passed!' Amy was jubilant. By gaining her 'C' licence she became the first woman to qualify in Britain as a ground engineer and, at that time, the only woman in the world to hold a valid Ground Engineer's Licence.

It was true that Lady Heath, a pioneer aviator, had earlier obtained her ground engineer's licence in the United States. However, she had, as Amy told her mother in a letter, 'let her tickets lapse', and so Amy could rightly make her claim.

As far as aviation was concerned, Amy was proud and determined, as well as thorough. She continued to study for more licences and gained her Ground Engineer's 'A' licence early in 1930. This, coupled with her 'C' licence, enabled her to become an Associate Member of the Royal Aeronautical Society.

One day, while chatting to Captain Baker and Jack Humphreys, Amy bemoaned the difficulties of a woman being accepted as an aviator. Captain Baker commented that a woman aviator needed to do something outstanding.

'What?' queried Amy.

'Something like flying to Australia,' came the reply.

The conversation was casual and the remark light-hearted, but Amy thought deeply about it.

Ever since the Wright Brothers' achievement in 1903, aviators had tried to open up airways across the world. Their planes were flimsy, lightweight machines with open cockpits and only basic navigational aids. They had no contact with any air control if they should come down in some barren spot.

Adventurous pilots were offered ten thousand pounds if they could cross the Atlantic ocean in a plane. Several tried and failed, then, in 1919, John Alcock and Arthur Whitten Brown successfully made the flight in fifteen hours, fifty-seven minutes. They became heroes and, in addition to winning the money, were knighted.

Other airmen became keen to be the first to cover long distances between continents. In 1919 also, two Australian brothers, Keith and Ross Smith, flew from England to Australia. Their journey took twenty-seven days, twenty hours. Alan Cobham did the trip there and back in a seaplane in 1926 and two years later Bert Hinkler flew solo to Australia in a land plane in the record time of fifteen and a half days.

Amy considered the matter. There was a rush to make new records; soon there would be nothing new left to do. So far, men had made most of the record-breaking flights, although a few women had become famous aviators. Lady Heath made the first flight by a woman from South Africa to England, while Lady Bailey became the first woman to fly from England to South Africa and back. Amelia Earhart, an American, had flown the Atlantic, but as a passenger and not the pilot.

Amy made up her mind. She would be the first woman to fly solo from London to Australia and she would try to beat Hinkler's record.

In January 1930, a reporter from the London Evening News requested an interview with 'the lady mechanic'. To his surprise, Amy was as dirty and oil-stained as the men. He asked about her plans to fly to Australia, and the next day's paper boldly featured the story. Amy was infuriated because she was reported to be making a comfortable living as an aircraft mechanic when the truth was that she had earned nothing at all.

Amy's letters to her father regarding the proposed flight to Australia became very frequent and he gave her sound business advice. Amy calculated that it would cost one thousand pounds to buy a plane and finance the flight. She was determined to raise the cash somehow, although she had no money of her own. Letters asking for help were written to many influential people, including the Australian High Commissioner and the Australian Minister of Trade and Customs. Some people seemed mildly interested, but none were prepared to provide money. Amy tried to sell her story to a newspaper, even for a sum as low as £25, but not one would buy it. She approached Lord Wakefield, whose firm sold oil and petrol, and asked him to provide fuel for her Australian flight, but he would not agree.

Amy did something she had resolved she would never do; she asked her father to finance the Australian project. Mr Johnson's answer was a definite 'No!'

Both her father and her mother were now concerned about Amy's health. The strain of taking examinations and the stress of planning the flight to Australia had sapped Amy's strength. It would be suicide to try to fly the 11,000 miles to Australia at present. Amy assured them that she would not take unnecessary risks and promised to make her motto 'Be careful'. Slow down, advised her parents, recover your health and try later.

Stubborn as ever, Amy would not listen. At this time, Sir Sefton Brancker was the Director of Civil Aviation and addressed a meeting at the Royal Aeronautical Society. Amy was there and heard him urge British youth and the aviation industry to wake up and do something enterprising before other nations outstripped Britain in aviation achievement.

Amy was inspired. The words strengthened her determination and she wrote a long letter to Sir Sefton. She listed her qualifications, ambitions and the need for money to sponsor her Australian flight, but in one thing she was careless — she forgot to sign the letter! However, Sir Sefton was so impressed that he lost no time in tracing Amy.

Before she received his reply and less than three weeks before the planned flight to Australia, Amy heard that a Gipsy Moth plane was to be sold by Captain W L Hope. The aircraft was about two years old and had been fitted with extra fuel tanks for long distance flying. The price was £600.

Amy badly wanted the plane, so again she appealed to her father and this time he agreed to pay. Because she was eager to discuss matters with her father, Amy flew home to Hull from London piloting a flying club plane. The journey of 150 miles was the longest she had so far undertaken.

When Sir Sefton Brancker replied, he announced that Lord Wakefield would provide finance and Amy now knew that her Australian flight was a reality. With the money assured, Amy worked hard to prepare. She packed spare parts, tools, tyres, provisions, clothes and other necessities into the machine. Captain Hope advised her to take a revolver and a mosquito net, as well as medicines, first aid supplies and a portable cooker. Everything had to be squeezed into the little aircraft, and there was no room for the spare propeller. Amy solved the problem by tying it with rope to the side of the plane.

Amy called her fragile biplane 'Jason', the trade name of her father's fish firm. Remembering that Jason was heavily laden, Amy planned in detail her route to Australia. She studied maps and found some of them covering remote countries were very sketchy. She decided against taking the route Hinkler had flown and chose to travel in straight lines. Vienna, Constantinople, Baghdad, Bandar Abbas, Karachi, Allahabad, Calcutta, Bangkok, Singapore, Sourabaya, Atamboea, Port Darwin. These were to be twelve stopping points. The flight over Europe should be straightforward, with good landing places and efficient crews to re-fuel and service Jason. After India, the journey was across remote areas, including jungle and ocean.

Amy on the runway at Croydon

Amy checked her papers. The permit to land in Turkey had not arrived, nor had confirmation that petrol supplies would be available to cover the dangerous crossing of the Timor Sea. Everything else was ready, so Amy decided to leave as planned.

With no publicity and few people to see her go, Amy Johnson took off from Croydon Airport early on 5th May 1930.

4 Solo Flight

1st Day   5th May 1930   Croydon to Vienna
Amy flew over the English Channel in the wooden, cloth-covered frame of Jason, but whenever she pumped petrol, sickening fumes filled the cockpit and she nearly turned back. However, she persevered and when she reached Vienna in the late afternoon, efficient aircraft mechanics took charge of Jason. Amy was taken to the home of a friendly caretaker, who promised to wake her at 4 a.m. the next morning.

2nd Day   6th May   Vienna to Constantinople (Istanbul)
Heavy rainstorms battered the cockpit, but the 800 mile journey ended safely one hour before sunset. How different from Vienna! Here in Turkey few planes were seen and Amy insisted on servicing Jason herself, although it took five hours.

Volunteers tried to put Jason into a hangar but not realising the lightness and fragility of the craft, they pushed roughly until suddenly Jason tilted on to its nose. Fortunately, Amy had placed the propeller in the horizontal position, so no damage was done. A rope was brought and tied to Jason's upright tail, then the men gently pulled it back to the ground.

With Jason safely in a hangar, Amy met the Turkish authorities. Because her permit had not reached England in time, Amy carried letters of introduction from Sir Sefton Brancker to two notable Turkish gentlemen. After a lengthy search, the two gentlemen could not be found, but another Turk was persuaded to sign Amy's papers. The overnight delay caused precious hours to be lost.

3rd Day   7th May   Constantinople to Aleppo (Halab)
It was 10 a.m. before Amy left. Baghdad could not be reached in daylight, so she planned to stop at Aleppo, nearly 600 miles away. The treacherous Taurus mountains were shrouded in thick cloud and when the sun suddenly burst through, to her horror Amy saw Jason's wing-tip almost touch the rock face of a

'Jason'

mountain. By comparison, the remaining journey over the desert seemed easy, and Amy landed safely at Aleppo in Syria.

4th Day   8th May   Aleppo (Halab) to Baghdad

The 500 mile journey across desert began early. Amy was well on the way when, without warning, the temperature soared, Jason lost height and she could see nothing. Amy was enveloped in a sandstorm. Even though she wore protective goggles, sand irritated Amy's eyes. Jason's engine clogged, Amy lost control and the plane came down with a series of bumps. She pulled Jason round to face into the forceful wind and used her luggage as wedges and anchors. The wind snatched at the canvas engine cover, but with determination Amy fastened it, then sat on Jason's tail to prevent the plane rising. She was hot and exhausted and had no idea where she was. After three hours, the storm ceased. Miraculously, the engine started, and Amy's uncanny sense of direction enabled her to fly straight to Baghdad. Had she gone the wrong way, she would never have been seen again.

At Baghdad aerodrome, Jason tilted on one wing because an undercarriage strut had broken, probably during the emergency landing. A replacement could not be obtained, so mechanics at an Air Force aerodrome worked through the night making a new one.

Amy was treated like a queen. She was driven round the mystical city of Baghdad with its fairy-tale domes and minarets and escorted to a riverside dinner. What a contrast to the desert!

30

5th Day   9th May   Baghdad to Bandar Abbas

Amy left at 6 a.m. wearing borrowed cotton shorts instead of her heavy flying suit. As she followed the River Tigris she began to wonder if she could beat Bert Hinkler's eight day record from London to Karachi. Newsmen began to wonder, too, and followed her progress carefully.

The heat was unbearable. It affected Jason's engine and burned Amy's face. Over Bandar Abbas in Persia (now known as Iran), Amy could not find the aerodrome, so landed on a large, open space. The uneven ground damaged the bolt holding the new strut, and as Jason's wing trailed along the ground, tears pricked Amy's eyes.

A man emerged from a large house. He was the British Consul and explained that the airport was no longer used.

Amy felt unwell, so the Consul's wife took her into the cool house to rest. After being assured that David, who looked after the Consul's car, could cope with Jason, Amy fell asleep.

She awoke refreshed, but found Persian officials waiting to examine her papers.

'Where is your health certificate?'

Amy did not have one. Would these foreigners delay her departure from Bandar Abbas? She controlled her anger and argued courteously for two hours. Eventually, the officials accepted that as she would be in Persia only a very short time, she could not spread disease.

Amy wandered into the cool, moonlit night to service

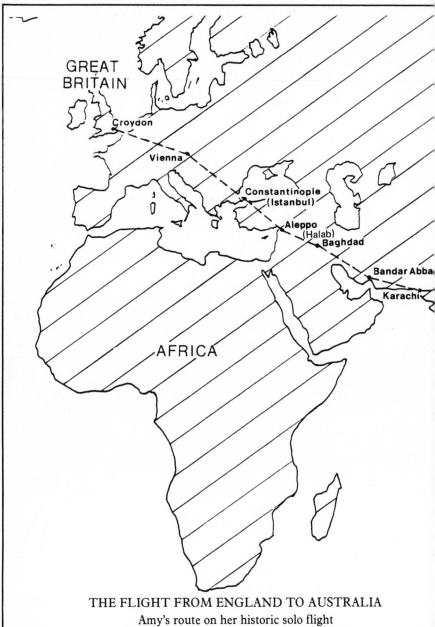

GREAT
BRITAIN

Croydon

Vienna

Constantinople
(Istanbul)

Aleppo
(Halab)

Baghdad

Bandar Abba

Karachi

AFRICA

THE FLIGHT FROM ENGLAND TO AUSTRALIA

Amy's route on her historic solo flight
from England to Australia. The names given
are those used in 1930 when the flight was
made. Where the name has changed, the
new one is given in brackets.

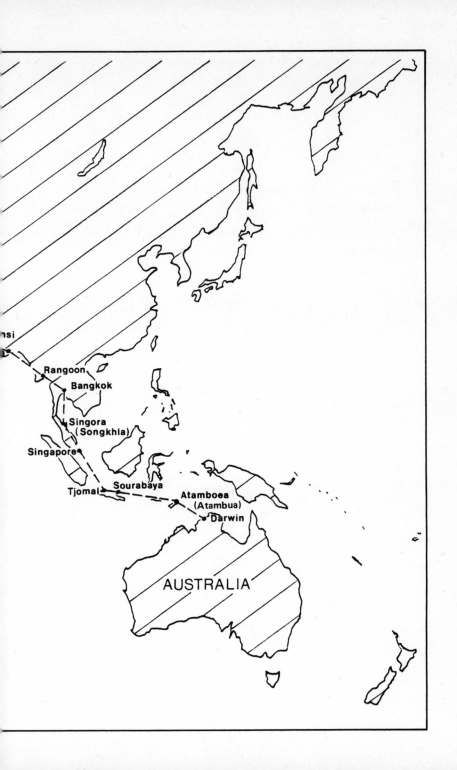

nsi

Rangoon

Bangkok

Singora
(Songkhla)

Singapore

Tjomal

Sourabaya

Atamboea
(Atambua)

Darwin

AUSTRALIA

Jason. David had repaired the damage and waited to help. Sand was everywhere and by the time everything was in good order it was 2.30 a.m.

6th Day   10th May   Bandar Abbas to Karachi

After only two hours sleep, Amy flew 700 miles over rough hilly country and turbulent waters. Something seemed wrong with Jason's engine, but she landed safely at Karachi in Pakistan, beating Bert Hinkler's London to Karachi record by two days!

The world went wild and waited to see if Amy could snatch the London to Australia record as well. Enthusiastic crowds rejoiced while Amy, excited but cautious, checked Jason. She knew immediately why the engine was not running smoothly. David had put an extra washer on the plug he repaired, which caused a short circuit that could have resulted in a fire. How lucky she had been to land safely! While others celebrated her achievement, Amy decided it was wiser to go to bed. She must not lose the chance to reach Australia more quickly than Bert Hinkler did.

5   Aiming for Australia

7th Day   11th May   Karachi to Jhansi
Amy, garlanded with flowers, left Karachi intending to
fly to Allahabad in India. But with 200 miles still to
complete, the daylight faded and little petrol remained,
so Amy attempted to land in a clearing. Jason careered
past trees, narrowly missed a telegraph pole and became
wedged between two buildings. Men scattered, then
raced to help Amy as the plane stopped. She had landed
at the Indian Army Barracks, Jhansi. Fortunately, the
damage was less than first thought, and experts
willingly carried out repairs.

8th Day   12th May   Jhansi to Calcutta
After stopping at Allahabad to re-fuel, Amy flew to
Calcutta on the Ganges Delta, 650 miles away. She
arrived hot and tired, but could relax because Jason
was in the hands of efficient staff who carried out all the
necessary checks, adjustments and servicing. Amy went
to bed determined to make an early start the next
morning. What began as a happy adventure was now a
serious mission.

9th Day   13th May   *Calcutta to Rangoon*

'The monsoon may break soon,' Amy was warned as she made a dawn start. She could not delay, so flew high over mist-covered mountains and jungle. Dropping lower, she just glimpsed the railway line she needed to follow when huge black clouds released torrential rain. The dreaded monsoon had broken. Water streamed over Amy's goggles so that she could not see. Where was Rangoon Racecourse, her landing point? Swooping in circles, she made out a track. This must be it!

Too late, Amy realised her mistake as Jason staggered past goal posts and, with a loud crack, tipped into a ditch. This was the sports field of Insein Engineering Institute. Jason, with a broken propeller and under-carriage strut, a ripped tyre and damaged wing, was carried to shelter from the raging monsoon. It took three days to fit the spare propeller and carry out repairs. The sports field was too small for take-off, so Jason was towed several miles to Rangoon Racecourse by the local fire engine.

12th Day   16th May   *Rangoon to Bangkok*

The monsoon still raged as Amy flew over the mountains, so that a distance normally covered in thirty minutes took three hours. Amy lost her way, but when she saw towers of temples among glittering palaces and pagodas, she knew she had reached Bangkok, the capital city of Siam (the country now called Thailand).

Excited crowds jostled to greet Amy, but as soon as she could get away, she went to Jason's hangar. Airport personnel, trying to help, had done all the wrong things, so Amy had to start again and service Jason herself.

13th Day   17th May   Bangkok to Singora (Songkhla)
At first blinding rain prevented Amy from seeing properly, but eventually the weather cleared and Amy checked her position. She was only half way to Singapore where she intended to land and it was too late to complete the remaining 450 miles. No one was there to help as she made an unscheduled stop at Singora, but as soon as the news spread, curious crowds brought picnics and ice-cream to eat as they watched Amy work on her plane.

The people were so inquisitive that an area had to be roped off to keep them a safe distance from Jason. Amy waited until the cool of evening before servicing Jason. As she struggled to turn an obstinate nut and bolt, the crowd pushed a strong man forward to help her. After that, whenever Amy appeared to be in difficulty, the people chanted, 'Strong man, strong man', until the huge man appeared and gave his assistance.

14th Day   18th May   Singora (Songkhla) to Singapore
People still clustered round Jason as Amy prepared for early-morning take-off. She sighed with relief as Jason rose into the air without causing casualties.

A change of course was necessary to avoid bad weather, but otherwise the journey was uneventful. When Amy saw several aircraft flying towards her she wondered what was happening. The planes gathered in formation and proudly escorted her to Singapore.

Amy about to set off in her repaired aeroplane

Well-dressed Europeans cheered as Amy, with an oil-streaked, sunburnt face, stepped from her plane. Messages of congratulation awaited her, but Amy now knew she could not beat Hinkler's Australia record.

15th Day 19th May Singapore to Tjomal
Amy aimed to travel the 1,000 miles to Sourabaya, Java, in one day, but again stormy weather delayed her. She was terrified as she tried to take a short cut across the shark-infested Java Sea, so kept to the coast and, as daylight faded, intended to land on the sandy beach. She changed her mind as she saw a large, flat area and

came down, but Jason's fabric was torn by bamboo poles sticking out of the ground. The poles marked the plot of a house to be built near the sugar factory in Tjomal. Amy searched through her first-aid kit and stuck Jason's fabric together with sticking plasters meant to bind cut fingers.

16th Day   20th May   Tjomal to Sourabaya
Jason was refuelled at Semarang, where Amy accepted a Dutch pilot's offer to show her the way to Sourabaya. Trying to keep up with the powerful mail plane put a strain on Jason's engine and Amy was too worried about her plane to fully appreciate Sourabaya's lavish welcome. The propeller airscrew was wearing and Amy could do nothing about it. Nothing, that is, until an anonymous gift arrived. The owner of a Moth sent *his* airscrew to be fitted to Jason. Repairs lost a day's flying, but Amy was always grateful for the gift.

18th Day   22nd May   Sourabaya to Atamboea (Atambua)
The journey of 925 miles crossed dangerous seas and sparsely inhabited islands. Amy had little idea of the distance she flew through thick cloud and over stormy water. As the journey dragged on, Amy became exhausted. Only the noise of Jason's engine broke the monotony as she covered endless miles. Would she ever reach Australia?

AMY JOHNSON MISSING!

London papers proclaimed the news and the story flashed round the world. When Amy did not arrive at

Atamboea, ships and flying boats organised a search for her.

What *had* happened? Amy, her petrol tanks empty, had come down at Haliloeli in Timor, in a field with anthills as high as men. Without warning, a group of men brandishing spears surrounded Jason. Amy clutched her revolver as their leader stepped forward. The fearsome-looking man spoke, but Amy could not understand him, so she bravely smiled. He led her along rough paths to a white-bearded figure — the Dutch minister of the tiny church. The Minister and Amy conversed in halting French and the simple meal he provided tasted like a royal banquet.

An unexpected noise made Amy look up. Why should a car horn sound in the jungle? The Commander of Atamboea Airport had arrived to tell Amy she had flown twelve miles too far!

Amy returned to Atamboea to find that petrol supplies had not arrived. Some rusty drums were found, but by the time Amy had filtered the poor quality fuel they contained, she had lost another day's flying.

20th Day   24th May   Atamboea (Atambua) to Darwin
Australia was now just 485 miles away across the Timor Sea. The journey was so monotonous that Amy avoided looking at her watch too often. Jason spluttered. A jet had become choked with grit from the dirty petrol. Amy opened up the throttle and after several attempts blew it clear.

Half way along the route, the Shell tanker 'Phorus'

40

was looking out for Amy. Sailors cheered as Jason's registration letters G AAAH came into view. Amy swooped low to greet the ship then, noting the wind direction by the smoke from its funnel, adjusted her course and flew on.

Soon she would reach Australia. A black cloud loomed up on the horizon. Was it bad weather ahead? No! This was not cloud, but land — Australia! Amy had accomplished what she set out to do.

Triumphantly, on 24th May 1930, Amy Johnson became the first woman to fly solo half-way round the world, from London, England to Darwin, Australia.

6 Amy, Wonderful Amy

Amy arrived in Darwin to the kind of welcome that today is only given to pop stars. People were wild with excitement. Amy was very tired, but pleasantly surprised when, only a few hours after landing, she attended a reception in Darwin Town Hall. The Australians adored her for her simplicity and unaffected manner.

Brisbane was the next stop, but Amy landed badly, causing Jason to hit a fence and somersault. Onlookers gasped with relief as Amy crawled unhurt from the badly damaged plane. It was decided that she should be a passenger as she flew to visit Sydney, Melbourne, Adelaide and Perth.

Amy was taken to Sydney in an Australian National Airways plane. One of the crew, a stranger named James Mollison, made Amy promise to dance with him twice at that night's ball. The promise was never fulfilled because, when Mollison asked for her, Amy's host said she was too tired. Amy often wondered why the handsome co-pilot never claimed his dances.

Organisations of every size and kind demanded that Amy should speak to their members and Amy was whisked from one event to another. She received more letters, telegrams and messages of congratulation than she could cope with. Over the radio came the strains of songs composed in her honour, especially one called 'Amy, Wonderful Amy'. Movietone newsreels whirred as Amy's filmed exploits were shown in cinemas. Poets competed with each other to put their praises of Amy into verse. Amy chuckled at the caption beneath one cartoon which read, 'Our Amy has got more backbone than her father's kippers'.

Gifts were showered on Amy — jewellery, watches, fur coats, silver trays and numerous other items. There was no time to enjoy these, for she had to fit interviews, broadcasts, photo sessions and other tasks into every spare minute. In public, Amy's smile won people's hearts, but in private she often shed tears because she longed to escape from the publicity.

People celebrated Amy's victory in unusual ways too.

Enthusiastic crowds greet Amy in Darwin, Australia

Amy waving to crowds in London

The children of New South Wales, Australia, gave Amy some money. With it she bought a gold cup to be awarded annually to a child for an act of courage. In England, The Daily Sketch asked people to contribute to a 'Shilling Fund' (5p) to buy Amy a new aeroplane.

News came from England that she had been made a

CBE (Commander of the British Empire) and when she returned home King George V presented her with the honour at Buckingham Palace.

Back in England, an ecstatic official welcome awaited her at Croydon Airport. Excited crowds packed the streets to watch Amy pass along the twelve mile route to London and at midnight countless enthusiasts cheered as she appeared on a hotel balcony.

Not to be outdone, her home town of Hull gave Amy a welcome which lasted three days. Numerous other towns and different societies made awards and presentations to her. She was particularly pleased when the Society of Engineers invited her to speak about the performance of Jason's engine.

The Daily Mail gave Amy £10,000. It was not an outright gift, and in return for the money Amy had to take part in a strenuous publicity tour. She was required to visit forty towns in a period of three months, making public appearances and speaking about her flight.

She soon rebelled against being a celebrity. The publicity got out of hand and went sour. Amy felt like a puppet as she opened bazaars and put in brief appearances to aid charities. She wanted to help, but the strain overcame her and The Daily Mail agreed to release her from such duties.

Amy had a severe nervous breakdown and her recovery was slow, but she desperately longed to fly again. Where could she go? Amy quietly made her plans, recovered her health and was happy.

Her first ideas had to be abandoned but Amy was not discouraged. She flew to Tokyo in a plane that had a cabin instead of an open cockpit. Jack Humphreys, the Chief Engineer at Stag Lane, accompanied her. They arrived in Moscow late at night on 28th July 1931. It was the first time anyone had flown from London to Moscow in one day. Continuing an uneventful journey, Tokyo was reached in just under ten days, breaking by just one day the record set up by a Japanese pilot. Amy was given a rapturous welcome but the achievement did not receive excessive world-wide publicity.

The limelight was stolen by a solo flight from Australia to England which had taken just nine days — a miraculously short time in 1931. The aviator was James Mollison. Amy remembered him as the co-pilot with whom she promised to dance, and sent him a message of congratulation.

On returning to England, Amy began a lecture tour but was suddenly taken ill. 'Amy Johnson has Appendicitis!' announced the newspapers. She had an operation and, after a few weeks, set sail on a cruise to recover her health.

While Amy was ashore in Cape Town, South Africa, James Mollison landed there from England in the first light plane to make the journey by crossing the Sahara desert. Standing in the crowd, Amy could see he was exhausted. He had slept for only two hours in nearly five days.

Before Amy rejoined her ship, she and Jim lunched together. Amy knew Jim was a flatterer, adored by many young ladies. He enjoyed a social life that was not part of Amy's world, but he was an outstanding

Amy and Jim on their wedding day

pilot and she could converse with him about flying. No wonder Amy lost her heart to the man who called himself 'The Playboy of the Air'.

They did not meet often but later, when they were both in London, Jim took Amy to lunch at a fashionable restaurant. Amy noticed the expensively dressed society people and knew she did not fit in. She was a simple Yorkshire girl who loved flying. Jim, realising that Amy felt uncomfortable, reassured her.

Quite suddenly, towards the end of the meal, Jim asked Amy to marry him and shortly afterwards, on 29th July 1932, their wedding took place. Crowds besieged the church and the only people, it seemed, who were not informed were Amy's parents. She did not let them know until the last moment and the family made an overnight dash from Yorkshire to London, but only arrived at the end of the ceremony.

7 Tragedy

Amy and Jim snatched an idyllic honeymoon in a remote Scottish castle but, because Jim was soon to attempt to fly from Ireland to America, it lasted only a few days. He wanted to be the first to make the east to west solo crossing of the Atlantic. Amy and Jim made a pact that their marriage would not interfere with either of their flying careers.

Jim began the journey in his new Puss Moth plane which he called 'Hearts Content' after the Newfoundland village where he hoped to land. Amy bravely waved goodbye — she knew how easily things could go wrong.

Jim successfully completed his flight, setting up four new records, and a few weeks later Amy attempted to break Jim's record from England to South Africa. She succeeded and also beat the record for the return journey and became the first solo pilot to fly from England to South Africa and back in record time. The achievement gained her the Segrave Trophy.

Amy was again very much in the public eye — adoring crowds, newspaper articles and placards said, 'Bravo, Amy!' Jim's achievements, too, were widely proclaimed, but Amy knew that he was jealous of her fame, though proud of her achievements. They had a winter holiday at St. Moritz and Amy tried to join in the kind of social life which Jim enjoyed. The Mollisons were so different. While Jim was a brilliant pilot, he was easy-going, impulsive and charming, but Amy was cautious, hard-working and rather reserved. Sometimes Amy worried about Jim's life-style, and especially the amount of alcohol he drank.

Jim was restless. He wanted to make the first air crossing of the South Atlantic from England to Brazil. Flying 'Hearts Content' he reached Brazil in three and a half days, breaking records and winning the Royal Aero Club's Britannia Trophy.

Amy and Jim did not relax but planned their next venture. Together they would attempt the world's long-distance record by starting from New York, flying to Baghdad and then returning to London.

But there was something else Amy longed to do. She wanted to be the first woman to fly the Atlantic from east to west. They agreed to *fly* to New York before starting the world long-distance record attempt.

On 8th June 1933, their black plane 'Seafarer' attempted to take off. It was heavily overloaded and the Croydon runway proved to be too short. 'Seafarer' bumped along uneven ground and crashed as the undercarriage collapsed. Amy and Jim were shocked but unhurt, and fortunately the 450 gallons (2046 litres) of fuel on board did not catch fire.

Undeterred, one month later the Mollisons tried again. Their plane taxied along a stretch of hard flat sand at Pendine, South Wales. Take-off was successful, and soon the crowds of onlookers were left behind.

Once over the ocean there were no landmarks or points of interest. Jim and Amy depended on compasses, sunset and sunrise to calculate their position. Once Amy spotted some icebergs and became alarmed in case they were well off course, but soon Newfoundland came into view. They had succeeded in flying across the Atlantic from east to west and Amy was the first woman to do so.

They flew on because Jim was determined to reach New York non-stop, but petrol supplies were low. Over Connecticut, fifty miles from New York, they realised that the fuel tanks were empty. Jim tried to land at Bridgeport Aerodrome, but overshot and crashed in the surrounding marshes. 'Seafarer' ploughed into the sodden ground and turned on its back.

Amy was injured, but where was Jim? She groped about in the wet marsh until she found him, face down and unconscious. The airport ambulance rushed them to hospital. Eager fans pounced on 'Seafarer', taking so

The wreckage of 'Seafarer'

51

many souvenirs that nothing remained except the plane's skeleton.

Jim needed thirty stitches in his face, while Amy had injured both hands, an arm and a leg. Even in their hospital room, Amy and Jim could not recover quietly. The press invaded their privacy to take photographs of them heavily wrapped in bandages and demanded information to publish in the newspapers. No account was taken of the need for the two casualties to rest.

Scarcely had Amy and Jim recovered when the celebrations began. New York staged a 'ticker-tape' welcome and showers of tiny pieces of paper drifted like snowflakes from the skyscrapers as they drove through the city. Jim had received his acclaim when he flew solo across the Atlantic the previous year, and now his wife received the most attention. In the carnival atmosphere the New Yorkers went wild.

Amy and Jim stayed at the home of Amelia Earhart, the American who the previous year had become the first woman to fly solo across the Atlantic in the opposite direction to Amy. Amy liked Amelia's calm unassuming attitude and was impressed by the serious work she did to further flying and women's interests. Amelia could cope with the publicity without it affecting her life and work.

Amy's life was very different. She lived in hotels instead of having a real home, and felt cheaply publicised and exploited. Keeping up with Jim's social set irritated her. Amy knew that her marriage was not really successful.

Their injuries healed, but both Amy and Jim were in

Amy and Amelia Earhart

a nervous state. Because Lord Wakefield generously promised to replace 'Seafarer', Jim returned to England while Amy remained in America. During his absence she kept up-to-date with rapidly advancing aircraft techniques by co-piloting an American airline plane on a timetabled flight. She also visited aircraft factories to study new aeronautical methods.

The new 'Seafarer' was shipped from England and, when Jim returned, preparations to break the world's long distance record began. Three times Amy and Jim tried to take off from Wasaga Beach in Ontario, Canada, but the huge, heavily laden plane never became airborne and they abandoned the flight.

Amy was not well. She needed to have an operation for a stomach ulcer. As she recovered, the couple had a holiday in Bermuda, before Jim returned to England, leaving Amy to convalesce in America.

Soon Jim sent a cable. There was to be an air race from England to Australia. Would Amy join him? Amy immediately said 'Yes', not merely because of the challenge of the flight, but because she hoped it would mend their troubled marriage.

The Mollisons started from Mildenhall in Suffolk. This was the first time they had taken part in a race and they were apprehensive. 'Black Magic' was a Comet, a fast twin-engined plane with all the latest developments including new types of undercarriage and propellers. It was difficult to fly, and earlier Jim had refused to let Amy handle it. Determined as ever, she insisted.

In the air, 'Black Magic' flew beautifully and the Mollisons reached Baghdad non-stop and went on to halve the existing record to Karachi. After that everything went wrong — poor take-offs, faulty compass readings and engine trouble. They could only watch others fly past to victory while they waited for spare parts.

Amy's life seemed to be in ruins. The age of pioneering flights was almost over and she longed to do some serious work for aviation. She tried representing an aircraft firm, flying passenger aircraft on scheduled flights and writing newspaper articles, but none of these activities lasted long.

In autumn 1935, Amy realised that her marriage to Jim had crumbled. Jim toured the world on his own and Amy concentrated on her career.

One idea particularly interested her. Her England to

54

South Africa record had been beaten and it was suggested that she should try to regain it by flying a British cabin monoplane called a Percival Gull. What a different plane from Jason, her fragile Moth!

Amy took off, but had to return for repairs. She tried again, starting on 4th May 1936, and flew down the west coast of Africa, completing the journey to Cape Town in three days six and a half hours. Once again she had beaten the record and was in the public eye. Amy returned via the east coast of Africa, stopping at modern airports which now operated regular scheduled services. Progress in aviation was noticeable, for here were comfortable hotels and well-run services.

Amy gained another distinction. She was the first person to fly to Africa along the west route and return by the east coast, breaking records in both directions. This achievement gained her the Royal Aero Club's gold medal.

Amy's public still adored her, but her private life became impossible and Amy divorced Jim. She spoke to the Press and requested that once again she be called Amy Johnson. A lot of the unhappiness and strain on the marriage, she told reporters, was caused by publicity and rumours, coupled with interference by the Press.

8   World War Two

The fairy tale had ended. Amy and Jim did not live together happily ever after. People read the newspaper announcement of their divorce and were no longer interested. At last, Amy was out of the public eye.

She lived in the country, first in the Chilterns and then in the Cotswolds, enjoying cycling, horseriding and gliding, but her time could not be spent entirely on recreation. Amy had already sold her fur coat and jewellery to raise money and she needed employment to provide a regular income.

While she sought work connected with flying, Amy wrote articles for various newspapers and began her book called 'Sky Roads of the World'. She applied for appointment with the Air Ministry, but was offered an office job at £5 a week and in disgust she turned it down. Only men were allowed to fly and this made Amy furious.

A troubled cloud hung over Europe because Hitler's armies were tramping across neighbouring countries. When Poland was invaded, conflict became inevitable. Britain and France honoured their promise to fight if Hitler's troops marched into Poland and World War Two was declared on 3rd September 1939.

Only two months before the war, Amy became a pilot with a Portsmouth aviation company doing work for the Army. When war broke out Amy and the other pilots were transferred to Cardiff. By 1939, aeroplanes had become a strategic weapon of war. Amy was happy as she flew dangerous missions to France, but she soon received the disappointing news that the Royal Air Force was to take over the company. This meant that, because Amy was a woman, she would not be allowed to fly. What could she do?

An Air Transport Auxiliary had been formed so that pilots too old or disabled to join the RAF could ferry planes between factories and airfields. At first, the usual 'men only' rule applied, but later a Women's Section was formed.

Amy wanted to serve her country and she wanted to fly, so she applied to join the Air Transport Auxiliary and was accepted. Among the small group of women pilots Amy was, for the first time for years, really happy. Flights were dangerous. No radio was carried in case the enemy should intercept messages. Skill was needed to avoid barrage balloons put up to snare air invaders. The increasing attacks by the Luftwaffe, the German air force, meant that pilots had to be vigilant to avoid being shot down.

Returning to base at Hatfield after delivering a plane could be equally hazardous. The effects of war gripped Britain and travel was difficult. Unheated trains rarely ran to time and often broke down. Amy frequently journeyed overnight by rail, tightly wedged with others in packed corridors. It was not an easy life.

Amy learned that Jim had also joined the ATA and was stationed at nearby Whites Waltham. They rarely met, but gave each other a friendly greeting when they did.

The German air attack on England increased. The blitz disrupted life, but the Air Transport Auxiliary continued to deliver planes to the RAF.

On 4th January 1941, Amy delivered a plane to Prestwick in Scotland and left in another aircraft, an Airspeed Oxford, for Kidlington in Oxfordshire. Visibility became poor, so when Amy refuelled at Squire's Gate, Blackpool, she decided to stay the night with her sister, Molly, who lived in the area.

Next morning, Amy waited at Squire's Gate airport until the weather was reasonably clear. Thick cloud was forecast for the south, the direction in which Amy was travelling, but she said, 'It's all right. I'll fly over the top'.

At ATA Hatfield later that day, the officer in charge was worried. Amy was overdue. Her flight should have taken one hour. She had left Squire's Gate at mid-morning and now it was late afternoon. A report came through that an Oxford aircraft had come down in the Thames Estuary. A tiny figure was seen parachuting into the water and two bags labelled 'A. Johnson' had been found.

What had happened to Amy, whose motto was 'Be Careful'? Had the plane's wings iced up in the bitter weather? Why was she well off course? Did her compass give wrong readings? Overhead gunfire had been reported in the area, so was Amy shot down by an enemy plane? Jim Mollison was convinced that this happened. Did Amy collide with another plane? Did she run out of petrol or have engine trouble?

No one knows, and the reports of the crew of a naval vessel which attempted a rescue only complicated matters. HMS Haslemere was patrolling in the Herne Bay area when the small figure of a woman, dangling from a parachute, descended from the clouds. As the parachute hit the water, Commander Fletcher jumped into the rough sea, but the ship heaved and the woman disappeared beneath the water. The crew said that another figure appeared and Commander Fletcher attempted a further rescue, but before he could do anything he had to be taken from the sea and later died.

Who was this second person? Was he an enemy pilot? *Was* it human, or merely baggage or wreckage from Amy's plane? We shall never know.

Rumour and counter-rumour persisted, but only one thing was certain. Although her body was never recovered, Amy Johnson, Britain's foremost woman aviator, gave her life for her country in World War Two.

Amy once predicted that she would drown in the sea. She often thought about the future and, to her, nothing was impossible. She foresaw regular airline flights and suggested that passengers should either be given sleeping tablets or provided with entertainment to overcome the boredom of a tedious flight. Amy realised that it would be essential to have pressurised air-conditioned passenger cabins. In the late 1930s, less

Amy — the pioneering pilot

than forty years after the first powered flight, Amy toyed with the idea that, perhaps in a hundred years' time, man might fly to the moon.

She trod an unsteady path through life, making mistakes and never coming to terms with being famous. She could be obstinate and was not a perfect pilot. It was her courage, determination and love of adventure which enabled her to be the first woman to fly solo from England to Australia in a fragile Gipsy Moth biplane she called 'Jason'.

'Jason' was bought by Lord Rothermere for the nation and can now be seen at the Science Museum in South Kensington, London.

In 1959, Amy's other trophies and mementoes were donated by her father to Bridlington Corporation, Yorkshire, who made a special 'Amy Johnson Room' in Sewerby Hall Art Gallery and Museum. Here, displayed for all to see, are photographs and many other things connected with Amy — her flying suit, the CBE decoration, a Japanese kimono, an Australian boomerang and much more.

Amy was an unassuming young woman who longed to do something for others and for England. Her exploits were not mere record-breaking gimmicks, but a major contribution to establishing passenger air routes all over the world.

She was, and always will be,

Amy, Wonderful Amy.